The Battle

"How's your time capsule project coming along?" Mr. Wakefield asked.

"My team's got two terrific things already," Elizabeth announced. "All we need is one more. And if we can get what we think we might get, we'll be a shoo-in."

Jessica glared at her. Then she beamed at her father. "My team's got great things, too."

"That's good," Mr. Wakefield said. "I'm glad to see this isn't turning into a battle between the two of you."

"Oh, no," Elizabeth said. "Nothing like that."

"There's no battle," Jessica echoed, looking at her sister. Not yet, she thought.

Bantam Skylark Books in the SWEET VALLEY TWINS series
Ask your bookseller for the books you have missed.

SWEET VALLEY TWINS

Claim to Fame

Written by
Jamie Suzanne

Created by
FRANCINE PASCAL

A BANTAM SKYLARK BOOK®
TORONTO · NEW YORK · LONDON · SYDNEY · AUCKLAND

RL 4, 008–012

CLAIM TO FAME
A Bantam Skylark Book / October 1988

*Sweet Valley High® and Sweet Valley Twins are
trademarks of Francine Pascal.*

Conceived by Francine Pascal.

Cover art by James Mathewuse.

*Produced by Daniel Weiss Associates, Inc.,
27 West 20th Street,
New York, NY 10011*

*Skylark Books is a registered trademark of Bantam Books,
a division of Bantam Doubleday Dell Publishing Group, Inc.
Registered in U.S. Patent and Trademark Office and elsewhere.*

ISBN 0-553-15624-1

Published simultaneously in the United States and Canada

*Bantam Books are published by Bantam Books, a division of Bantam
Doubleday Dell Publishing Group, Inc. Its trademark, consisting of the
words "Bantam Books" and the portrayal of a rooster, is Registered in
U.S. Patent and Trademark Office and in other countries. Marca Regis-
trada. Bantam Books, 666 Fifth Avenue, New York, New York 10103.*

PRINTED IN THE UNITED STATES OF AMERICA

O   09876543

Claim to Fame

One

◇

"Elizabeth! Over here!"

Elizabeth Wakefield turned and saw her good friend Julie Porter beckoning to her. She made her way through the group of students chatting in the hallway between classes. "Hi!" she greeted Julie. "What's up?"

Julie's huge brown eyes were bright with anticipation. "I just heard there's going to be an assembly this period."

"I know," Elizabeth said. "It's got something to do with the middle school's twenty-fifth anniversary."

"Do you know what they're planning?"

Elizabeth shook her head. "No. But I've heard rumors that something really special is going to be announced."

"That's what I heard, too," Julie said. "When I

went by the principal's office I heard the secretaries talking about the assembly. They were saying something about a contest."

"What kind of a contest?"

"I don't know," Julie admitted. "But it's going to be part of the anniversary celebration."

"I wonder what a contest has to do with an anniversary," Elizabeth mused.

Other kids at school seemed to have heard the rumor about the contest too. As the two girls made their way down the hall, Elizabeth noticed several groups of students talking excitedly. She spotted her twin sister, Jessica, talking to her best friend, Lila Fowler.

"Maybe they know what's going on," Elizabeth said to Julie. "Hey, Jess, did you hear anything about the assembly this morning?"

Jessica nodded and exchanged a glance with Lila. They looked unusually smug. It was obvious that they knew something no one else knew.

Just then, Amy Sutton, Elizabeth's best friend, walked over and joined them.

"Hi, Amy. We're trying to pry some information out of Jessica," Elizabeth said.

"It's no big deal," Lila announced, looking bored. "It's just about that dumb twenty-fifth anniversary business."

"We *knew* that," Julie told her. "But I heard it's about some kind of contest, too."

"Oh, really?" Lila studied her fingernails casually. "What sort of contest?"

"Well, I guess we'll just have to find out when we get there," Elizabeth said. She had a strong suspicion that both Lila and Jessica knew a lot more than they were saying. But it was typical of Lila to want to keep the secret. It made her feel important.

"Lila always tries to act so cool," Amy whispered to Elizabeth and Julie as the took their seats in their classroom. "*I* don't think a twenty-fifth anniversary is dumb."

"Neither do I," Elizabeth whispered back. "I think it's neat! But you know how Lila is. . . ."

"Snobby," Amy broke in. Elizabeth wasn't that fond of Lila either, but Lila *was* Jessica's friend, so she had to be careful about what she said.

"I don't know why your sister hangs out with her," Amy mumbled.

"Well, they're both Unicorns, and Unicorns stick together," Elizabeth replied. The Unicorn Club was made up of a group of snobby girls who thought they were as special and as beautiful as the mythical beast for which their club was named. Just then, their teacher, Ms. Wyler, entered the room and began taking roll. Elizabeth sat quietly at her desk thinking about her twin sister.

Of course, it wasn't really surprising that she and Jessica had such different friends. They looked exactly alike on the outside, with the same long, blond hair, blue-green eyes, and a dimple in their left cheeks. But apart from that, they were complete opposites.

Elizabeth knew people thought of her as the more serious twin. She liked having fun and doing things with her good friends, but she also loved reading, writing, and spending time alone, just thinking.

Jessica, on the other hand, always liked to be the center of attention. She spent most of her free time with fellow members of the Unicorn Club, talking about clothes, makeup, and boys.

Elizabeth wasn't very interested in the Unicorn Club. Personally, she thought that most of the members were snobs. But she tried to be polite to them since they were Jessica's friends. In spite of all their differences, Jessica and Elizabeth were still the closest of friends and Elizabeth would never do anything to hurt her twin.

Elizabeth was jolted back into the present by the announcement that came over the intercom.

"Attention, all classes. Please proceed to the auditorium for a special assembly."

Elizabeth, Amy, and Julie joined the line of students filing out of the room. "Wow, this is great! We get to miss part of our class," Amy said. "I wonder if we'll find out what Sweet Valley Middle School was like twenty-five years ago. It was called Sweet Valley Junior High then," Amy informed them.

"How did you know that?" Julie asked.

"One of my mother's friends went to school here when it first opened," Amy replied. "She was a cheerleader."

"It must have been so different!" Elizabeth exclaimed.

Amy grinned. "I've even seen pictures of her when she was my age."

"What did she look like then?"

Amy giggled. "She had her hair all puffed up. She said all the girls used to tease their hair to get it like that. They called it 'ratting.'"

Julie made a face. "Ugh. That sounds gross!"

The girls entered the auditorium and took seats near the front. When everyone was settled, the principal, Mr. Clark, cleared his throat and spoke into the microphone on the stage.

"Good morning, students. I've called this special assembly today to tell you about a very exciting upcoming event. As you all must know by now, this year is the twenty-fifth anniversary of the opening of Sweet Valley Middle School. And I'm sure you'll agree with me that this is a cause for celebration."

"That's your opinion," hissed a voice behind Elizabeth. "Who wants to celebrate a school opening?"

Elizabeth didn't have to turn around to know it was Bruce Patman speaking. He was a conceited seventh grader who was always saying obnoxious things like that.

"We're kicking off the festivities," Mr. Clark continued, "with a dance next Friday to raise money for new softball dugouts."

Amy groaned. "A dance! I thought we were going to have a contest."

"Oh, come on, Amy. A dance will be fun," Elizabeth said enthusiastically.

Across the auditorium, Jessica Wakefield could hardly contain herself. The mere mention of a dance and she was already planning what she was going to wear.

"In honor of our anniversary," Mr. Clark went on, "this dance will have a sixties theme. We invite you to wear sixties clothes, dance to sixties music, and get the feel of what this school was like twenty-five years ago."

"Wow, this is going to be great," Jessica squealed excitedly. Lila nodded and murmured, "I think all the Unicorns should wear purple miniskirts."

Jessica agreed enthusiastically. Purple was the Unicorn official color and each member tried to wear something purple every day. Miniskirts would be fabulous!

"And," Mr. Clark continued, "we've got something very special planned. Mrs. Arnette, would you tell the students about your idea?"

The social studies teacher made her way up the stairs to the stage and over to the microphone.

Lila turned to Jessica and rolled her eyes. "I guess the Hairnet's going to tell us about the contest."

Jessica giggled. They called Mrs. Arnette "the Hairnet" because she always wore one.

The usually serious-looking teacher was smiling as she took the microphone. "As Mr. Clark told you, new softball field dugouts are going to be built. When the ground is broken to start construction, we're going to bury a time capsule, to be opened twenty-five years from now."

A murmur went through the auditorium and Mrs. Arnette rapped the podium for silence.

"I'm sure you're all wondering what's going to be placed inside the time capsule. Well, boys and girls, that's up to you. To make the collection of items as interesting and as varied as possible, we're going to hold a contest."

Jessica and Lila looked at each other and grinned.

Mrs. Arnette continued. "All students who would like to participate can team up in groups of four. Each team must find three items that symbolize the sixties, preferably from this school. The closer to the early sixties the better. Two weeks from tomorrow, a panel of teachers will decide which team has the most outstanding collection. The winners will get their pictures in *The Sweet Valley News*. And that's not all." She paused for a moment. "They will also have their photos placed in the time capsule."

Jessica already knew about this from Lila, who

somehow had a way of finding things out before anyone else. She turned to Lila. "Just think! Twenty-five years from now people will be looking at those pictures!"

Lila's eyes were gleaming. "And I know whose photos they'll be looking at! Ours!"

It was clear that a lot of other kids were having the same thought. As Mr. Clark dismissed the assembly, students began huddling together in groups and talking excitedly.

Ellen Riteman and Tamara Chase joined Jessica and Lila in the aisle. "We have absolutely got to win this contest," Lila informed them.

"If we can get our pictures in the time capsule, the Unicorns will have lasting fame," Jessica said happily.

Lila nodded and said, "Twenty-five years from now, when people find our pictures in the time capsule, they'll know we were the most important people at this school!"

"You're absolutely right, Lila," Ellen agreed. "This could make the Unicorns world famous!"

Tamara looked around the room. "It won't be easy coming up with the best stuff," she noted.

"Then we're just going to have to work harder," Jessica said excitedly. "Right?"

"Right," Lila said. "We'll have to find the best, most interesting things from the sixties. And we'll have to work fast to find them before anyone else does. After all, the reputation of the Unicorns is at stake!"

"This contest is going to be a lot of fun," Elizabeth said to Amy and Julie as they walked back toward their classroom. "I'll bet people come up with all kinds of interesting things."

"What sort of things were special in the sixties?" Amy wondered.

"A lot of people were hippies," Julie noted. "I saw an old photo in a scrapbook of my father playing a guitar. He had long hair, bell-bottom jeans, and he was wearing love beads!"

"Love beads!" Elizabeth tried to picture Julie's father wearing a necklace. It was impossible.

"Maybe he still has them," Amy said. "He could give them to us for the time capsule!"

Mrs. Arnette approached them. "Are you girls talking about the time capsule?"

Elizabeth nodded. "We're going to sign up for the contest as soon as we get a fourth person for our team."

"Well, I believe I've got a fourth person for you," Mrs. Arnette said.

"Who's that, Mrs. Arnette?" Julie asked.

"George Henkel," the teacher said. "I think it would be very nice if you girls invited him to join your team."

Elizabeth barely knew George, even though

they had a few classes together. He never spoke in class, and he didn't seem to have any friends. At least, whenever Elizabeth saw him, he was alone.

Mrs. Arnette was still standing beside them, waiting for an answer. Elizabeth spoke first. "I guess we could ask him to join us," she said. "Is that okay with you guys?"

"Sure," Julie said uncertainly. Amy just murmured, "OK with me."

Elizabeth knew they didn't sound terribly enthusiastic about the idea, but Mrs. Arnette was looking at them with approval. "We'll go ask him right now," Elizabeth said.

"I've never even noticed him before," Julie confessed in a whisper as the girls walked back to class.

"I'll bet he won't even want to do this," Amy added. "He doesn't seem like the type who would be interested."

"We'll never know unless we ask," Elizabeth said.

George didn't look up as they approached him. Elizabeth coughed to get his attention. When he saw them, he looked startled.

"Uh, George, we need a fourth person on our team for the time capsule contest. Would you like to join us?" Elizabeth asked.

He stared at them, as if he wasn't sure he'd heard her correctly. "You want me on your team?"

The girls nodded.

"Why?"

Elizabeth bit her lip and tried to think quickly. "Well, we thought it would be good to have someone who was in a class with us," she began. "So we could get together easily."

It wasn't much of a reason, and she didn't think George would buy it. But he just shrugged. "OK."

"Good!" Elizabeth said brightly.

George didn't say anything else, and they all just stood there awkwardly. Then Elizabeth thought of something.

"George, there's a Howard Henkel who doesn't live far from my house. Are you any relation to him?"

George stared at the floor for a minute. Then he nodded. "He's my father."

Elizabeth tried very hard not to look as surprised as she was. Mr. Henkel was a strange, reclusive man who was confined to a wheelchair. Elizabeth sometimes ran errands for him. And she'd never seen George there.

Amy didn't bother to hide her surprise. "You live near the Wakefields?"

"No," George said quickly. "My father does. I live with my aunt and uncle."

"Where's your mother?" Amy asked bluntly.

"She's dead," George replied.

There was another moment of awkward silence. "I guess we'd better sit down before the bell rings,"

Julie said. "When are we all going to get together?"

"Tomorrow's Saturday. Why don't we meet downtown," Elizabeth suggested. "How about one o'clock, in front of the drugstore?"

"OK," George said. Julie and Amy agreed, too.

Taking her seat at the front of the room, Elizabeth couldn't resist glancing back at George. She still couldn't believe George was Mr. Henkel's son. She'd never even seen George in the neighborhood.

The bell rang, and Elizabeth tried to concentrate on class. But it wasn't easy. All through class, she wondered about George. Why did he live with his aunt and uncle? Why didn't he live with his father?

Two
◇

The next morning, Jessica lay in bed and thought about the time capsule. It would be buried for twenty-five years. The kids who would open it weren't even born yet!

She closed her eyes and tried to picture Sweet Valley Middle School twenty-five years into the future. In her imagination, students were opening the time capsule, and one of them pulled out a photograph of Jessica.

"What a beautiful girl," one student exclaimed. "She must have been really important to get her picture in the time capsule!"

"Jessica! Last chance for breakfast!" Her mother's voice broke into her fantasy. Jessica sighed before pulling herself out of bed and throwing on a robe.

"I was wondering if you planned to spend the

day in bed," Mrs. Wakefield commented as Jessica strolled into the kitchen.

Jessica grinned. "No way! I'm meeting Lila, Tamara, and Ellen at the mall."

Her brother, Steven, was at the table, working his way through a heaping bowl of cereal. "Didn't you guys just go to the mall last week?" he asked. "The stores probably haven't even had time to restock their shelves yet."

Jessica ignored him. "Is Elizabeth still sleeping?" she asked her mother.

Her mother handed her a glass of juice. "No, your sister was up and out ages ago. Do you want cereal or eggs?"

Jessica looked at her mother in dismay. Was Elizabeth already out hunting with her team?

"She's out helping Mr. Henkel," Mrs. Wakefield continued.

Jessica made a face as she sat down at the kitchen table. "He gives me the creeps. He just sits in that wheelchair and looks mean. Why does Elizabeth go over there anyway?"

"Because she cares about people." Mrs. Wakefield placed a bowl of cereal in front of Jessica. "And I wouldn't call him mean, Jessica." She paused thoughtfully. "I think he looks sad."

Jessica shrugged. She had other things on her mind right now.

"Mom, who do you know who went to Sweet Valley Middle School when it first opened?"

Her mother wrinkled her brow. "Let me think about that."

"Did you save anything from where you went to school? Like, maybe cheerleading pom-poms?"

Mrs. Wakefield laughed. "Good heavens, no."

Steven looked at her curiously. "What do you want old cheerleading pom-poms for? Can't the school afford to buy new ones?"

Jessica rolled her eyes. "It's for our time capsule, dummy. We're having a contest at school to see who can bring in the three best items representing Sweet Valley Middle School in the sixties. And I just thought Mom could give me some good ideas."

"Is Elizabeth entering the contest, too?" Mrs. Wakefield asked.

Jessica nodded. "But we're on different teams." The minute those words left her mouth, she wished she could take them back. Knowing they were on different sides was going to give Steven a great excuse to tease them. Not that he ever needed an excuse. Before he could say anything, she turned pleading eyes to her mother. "Can you think of any good ideas for collecting stuff?"

"Well maybe I'll go through some of my old things in the basement when I have a chance."

"Thanks." Hastily, Jessica gulped down the rest

of her juice and finished eating her cereal. "I better go get dressed. See ya later, Mom."

An hour later, Jessica was hurrying into Casey's Place, an ice cream parlor at the mall. Lila, Ellen, and Tamara were already there, waiting for her in a booth. Jessica slid in next to Lila. "Sorry I'm late," she said breathlessly.

"You haven't missed anything," Lila told her. "We're trying to think of special things that have something to do with the sixties. Do you have any ideas?"

Jessica thought. "We could find some pictures of people back then. I know my mother has an old scrapbook."

Lila shook her head. "That's not special enough. We need things that will really impress the judges. Anyone can bring in old photographs."

"What about old clothes?" Ellen suggested.

"Everyone will be looking for old clothes for the dance," Jessica told her. "And they might use them for their time capsule collections too."

"We need things that are more original," Lila said firmly. "We've got to come up with stuff no one else has. Everybody, *think!*"

They sat there in silence, thinking. But no one came up with any brilliant ideas. A waitress came up to their table.

"What can I get you girls?"

Jessica was on the verge of suggesting hot fudge

sundaes, but Lila jumped up suddenly. "Nothing," she said to the waitress, turning to the others. "We're wasting time just sitting here. Let's walk around the mall and see if we get any ideas. It's much too early for ice cream, anyway."

Jessica and the others followed her out of the ice cream parlor. Once in the mall, they began strolling past the stores and looking in the windows. Tamara paused in front of a jewelry store.

"I've seen pictures of people wearing peace symbols around their necks," Jessica remarked. She scanned the window display, but she didn't see anything that looked like a peace symbol.

"Ooh, let's go in the poster shop!" Ellen exclaimed.

Lila looked at her in exasperation. "We're not going to find what we need in there."

"I know," Ellen said, "but I want a new poster for my bedroom. Can't we just go in there for a minute?"

Lila sighed. "OK, but just for a minute."

They were on their way across the mall to the poster shop when Jessica stopped suddenly. "Look," she whispered to Lila. "It's Bruce Patman."

Bruce sauntered toward them carrying a bag and looking very pleased with himself.

"Hi Bruce," Jessica called out sweetly. Behind her, Ellen and Tamara were giggling. "What are you doing here?"

"I'm meeting some of the guys," Bruce said. "We're just going to hang out."

"We're trying to find things for the time capsule," Jessica told him. Lila poked her in the ribs.

"And we've already found some wonderful things," Lila added quickly. "But don't ask us what they are because we're not telling."

Bruce grinned. "I don't even want to know. I just got something pretty fantastic for my team. This alone ought to get our pictures in the time capsule." He held up the bag, and the girls looked at it curiously.

To Jessica's surprise, Bruce opened the bag. "And I don't mind showing you, either. 'Cause you'll never find anything like this." He stuck his hand in the bag and pulled out an oddly shaped metal figure.

Jessica stared at it. "What's that?"

Bruce smirked. "It's the hood ornament from a Corvette Stingray. That was one of the most popular cars in the sixties, and they don't even make them anymore."

Jessica's heart sank. She knew what Bruce was holding could be a winning item. "Where'd you get it?"

"It's from one of my father's first cars," Bruce said. "He's been saving it all these years."

"And he's going to let you bury it in the time capsule?" Lila asked.

Bruce's smirk faded a little and he didn't look quite so confident. "Well, I haven't actually asked him yet. I just took it from his desk to show the guys."

Jessica gave Lila a reassuring look. She was sure Mr. Patman wouldn't want Bruce putting his hood ornament somewhere where he couldn't see it again for twenty-five years.

"That's very nice, Bruce," Lila said. "But I think maybe you'd better ask your father before you start bragging about winning the contest." She turned abruptly and headed for the poster store. Jessica managed to flash one quick smile at Bruce before following her. Bruce might be a showoff, but he was still pretty cute.

"His father will never go for that," Jessica said confidently as they entered the poster store.

"I'm not so sure about that," Lila said with less confidence. "Bruce is used to getting everything he wants."

Jessica stifled a laugh. If anyone got what she wanted, it was Lila—she was an only child and her father was one of the wealthier men in Sweet Valley. All Lila had to do was mention something once and she got it.

Tamara and Ellen paused to admire a poster of a rock star, while Jessica and Lila wandered toward the back, gazing at all the other posters.

"Oh, Lila, look," Jessica sighed. "It's a poster

from *Gone With the Wind*. Remember when we checked out that video?"

Lila didn't answer. She stared at the poster, and then her eyes widened, as if something had just occurred to her. Quickly, she called to a salesperson. "Do you have any movie posters from the 1960s?"

"Why, yes, we do," the man replied. "Any movie in particular?"

"No," Lila said. "But I'm looking for something that was very popular and *very* sixties."

The man smiled and went over to a special poster rack. Jessica and Lila followed him and waited while he flipped through the rack.

"Here's one you girls might like," he said. "I was a teenager when this film came out, and I can assure you, it was very popular."

"*Bikini Beach Party,*" Jessica read from the poster. The picture showed a group of teenagers on the beach. "Lila, this is perfect!"

"It's rather expensive," the man warned them. "You see, it's an original, not a reproduction. This actual poster was used in a movie theater, right here in Sweet Valley. It's a collector's item, so it costs quite a bit more than our usual posters."

Lila casually pulled out her father's credit card and said, "We'll take it."

Jessica hugged herself in glee. "Lila, this is great! I'll bet no one else comes up with an original movie poster!"

Ellen and Tamara joined them, and Lila and Jessica told them about their find. They all agreed it would be a perfect contribution to the time capsule.

"That's one down, two to go," Ellen noted. "What else can we get?"

Lila cocked her head to one side. "You know, I keep thinking about Bruce's hood ornament. I wonder if my father saved anything like that."

"I asked my mother, too," Jessica said. "She's checking."

"Let's go back to my house and see if my father has anything," Lila suggested. The salesman returned with the rolled-up poster neatly wrapped in brown paper, and the girls took off.

On the way back to Lila's, the girls talked about other possible items for the capsule. "What does Elizabeth have?" Lila asked Jessica.

"I don't think her team has started looking yet," Jessica said.

"I'll bet they're out looking today," Lila remarked. "Maybe you should sneak into her room when she's not there and take a look around."

"OK," Jessica said slowly, but she felt a little funny about spying on her own sister. Lila seemed to read her thoughts.

"Remember," she pointed out, "you're doing this for the Unicorns."

"I know, I know," Jessica said quickly. "I'll see what I can find out."

When they arrived at Lila's big house, Mrs. Pervis, the Fowlers' housekeeper, let them in. "Where's my father?" Lila asked her.

"He's not home at the moment, dear," Mrs. Pervis told her, and Lila frowned. She turned to the others. "Let's go in the den. He keeps a lot of stuff in there. Maybe we'll find something."

"Would you girls like some sandwiches and sodas?" Mrs. Pervis asked them as they trailed into the den.

"Yes," Lila yelled over her shoulder.

Jessica couldn't believe that Lila didn't even say thank you. If Mrs. Wakefield offered refreshments and Jessica didn't bother to thank her, they'd never see those sandwiches!

The den was a big room filled with lots of fancy stereo equipment. "You can put some records on," Lila called to the others.

Jessica began looking through the huge record collection. She had never heard of most of the names, but she found one album that was familiar.

"*Meet the Beatles*," she read from the cover. "I know this record. It was their first album. They still play it on the radio all the time." When she slid the record out from the sleeve, she noticed it was pretty scratched up. "This must be really old."

Lila gasped and whirled around. "The Beatles! They were big in the sixties!"

"And this must be an original record!" Jessica

exclaimed. "Lila, this is fantastic! My father told me the Beatles were the number one group when he was younger."

"It's perfect for the time capsule," Ellen said happily. "Would your father mind if we took it?"

"He'll never even notice that it's gone," Lila replied. "OK, now we've got two terrific things. All we need is one more."

"Any ideas?" Lila asked.

"I can still check with my mother," Jessica said. "Of course, if she does find something, I'll have to fight Elizabeth for it."

"Maybe you can bribe Elizabeth," Ellen suggested. "You could offer to do all her chores for the next month."

Jessica looked at her in shock. "All her chores?" She couldn't imagine anything more horrible.

"Remember," Lila reminded her, "you're doing this for the Unicorns, Jess."

"I know, Lila, but even if I offered to do all her chores, Elizabeth wouldn't agree."

"Well," Lila continued, "I still think you should find out what Elizabeth's team is up to."

"I will," Jessica assured her. She made a promise to herself that she would. Nothing was going to stop Jessica from winning now.

Three
◇

"There!" Elizabeth carefully wedged a bookend between two books and climbed down the small ladder. Then she stepped back to survey her work.

The new bookshelves reached almost to the ceiling, and practically every inch of them was covered with books. "It looks nice," she murmured.

"Very nice." Mr. Henkel gazed up at the shelves from his wheelchair and nodded in approval. "Thank you very much, Elizabeth. You're a big help."

"It was no problem," Elizabeth said cheerfully. "Who put the shelves up?"

Mr. Henkel gave a short, bitter laugh. "I have someone who comes in regularly to help out with the heavy work around the house."

A thought struck Elizabeth. "Mr. Henkel, how

are you going to get those books down from the upper shelves?"

Mr. Henkel pointed to a long pole with a clamp on one end leaning against the wall. "I use that."

"Oh." Elizabeth imagined Mr. Henkel struggling with the pole, trying to get a particular book off the shelf. And once again, she wondered why George didn't live here. Having someone around would certainly make life easier for Mr. Henkel, and there was plenty of room.

Of course, she couldn't ask him about that. She didn't want to seem nosy.

She looked at the shelves again. "You must read a lot," she noted.

Mr. Henkel grunted. "There's not much else I can do, is there."

It was more of a statement than a question, and Elizabeth didn't know what to say.

"Let me give you something for your work. . . ." Mr. Henkel began, breaking the uncomfortable silence.

Elizabeth shook her head vigorously. "No thanks, Mr. Henkel. I'm happy to help out." She couldn't remember how many times she'd said that to him. Every time she did something for Mr. Henkel he offered to pay her. And every time, she refused.

Mr. Henkel smiled slightly. "All right, Elizabeth." He sounded tired, and Elizabeth figured she'd better leave. She had to meet her team downtown anyway.

When Elizabeth turned to say goodbye to Mr. Henkel, she noticed that he was staring into space. Her heart ached for him.

Impulsively, she said, "Mr. Henkel, I know your son."

The man blinked and then looked at her. "What?"

"Your son, George. I know him. He's in some of my classes."

There was a moment of silence. "Oh," Mr. Henkel said finally. "Please close the door tightly behind you when you leave."

"OK," Elizabeth said. "Have a nice day, Mr. Henkel."

How strange, she thought, as she hurried downtown to meet the others. Mr. Henkel didn't even sound interested in his own son!

Julie and Amy were waiting for her in front of the pharmacy when she arrived downtown. "Hi," Elizabeth greeted them. "Where's George?"

"Here he comes now," Amy said. Elizabeth could see George walking slowly up the street. When he looked up and saw the girls, he quickened his pace.

"Am I late?" he asked when he reached them.

"No," Elizabeth assured him. "I just got here

myself." She paused and added, "I was helping your father put some books away. He just got some new shelves."

George didn't show any more emotion about his father than his father did about him. "Oh. Hey, I passed a secondhand shop on my way here. That might be a good place to start looking for things," George interrupted, changing the subject.

"Great idea," Julie said, and Elizabeth nodded in agreement. She was pleased to see George taking such an interest in the project. She was still curious about his relationship with his father, but she decided not to say anything more.

George led the group down the street and around the corner, to a little store called The Olde Junque Shoppe. Elizabeth had passed it before but she'd never looked at it closely. Now, peering in the small display window, she saw all kinds of interesting things.

"Look at that old-fashioned doll," she exclaimed. "It must be a hundred years old!"

"Wow. That does look old. I hope they have some newer stuff than that," Amy said. They went inside and Elizabeth looked around in fascination. Though it was a small shop, it was crammed full of the oddest assortment of things she'd ever seen.

"I'll look through these old magazines," Julie offered. "Maybe one of them is from the sixties." Just then, a gray-haired, jolly-looking woman emerged through curtains at the back of the shop.

"Can I help you?" she asked.

"Where do you have things from the 1960s?" Amy asked.

The woman laughed. "I'm afraid I'm not that organized! You'd better just browse and see what you can find."

Elizabeth was actually hoping she'd say that. She thought it would be more fun to poke around and discover something on their own than just to have something handed to them. Julie started going through the magazines, while the others explored the rest of the shop.

"Ooh, look over here!" Amy called out from the back. Elizabeth and George joined her. Amy was standing by a rack of clothes, and holding up a bright yellow, almost Day-Glo, minidress.

"I'll bet this is from the sixties," Amy said. "I've seen dresses like this in old pictures."

Elizabeth examined it. "But we can't know for sure if it was made in the sixties," she said. "I mean, there's no date on it or anything."

"Yeah, I don't think we should turn anything in for the time capsule unless we're sure it's authentic," George said.

Reluctantly, Amy agreed. "But I'll bet we can all find some clothes here to wear for the dance."

"I'm not planning to go to the dance," George said stiffly. Elizabeth wasn't surprised to hear that. She couldn't remember ever seeing George at a school function.

"I'm not crazy about dances either," Amy confided. "But I thought this one might be fun."

George just shrugged. "I'm going to look over there," he mumbled, and went toward the other side of the shop.

"He's kind of strange, isn't he?" Amy whispered to Elizabeth.

"I don't think he's strange, exactly," Elizabeth replied. She was thinking about the look in George's eyes. It was the same look she'd seen just that morning, in his father's eyes. "I'm going to check out that box over there."

She turned away from Amy and started going through a box of old books. Some of the covers were so faded she couldn't even read them, but one of them caught her eye. She could just make out the title beneath a thick layer of dust: *American Literature*. She opened it and almost yelped.

Stamped on the inside cover were the words "Sweet Valley Junior High." Under that was the handwritten signature of the student who had used the book. And next to the name, there was a date— exactly twenty-five years ago!

"Hey, everyone look!" Elizabeth held the book

in the air as George, Julie, and Amy came toward her. "This textbook is from the very first year Sweet Valley Junior High was opened!"

"Oh, wow!" Amy squealed. "That's perfect!"

"And it's not just some ordinary object from the sixties," Elizabeth said, her voice ringing with glee. "It's from *our* school!"

Even George seemed pleased.

As if on cue, the gray-haired woman emerged through the curtains again. "Have you kids found something?" she asked.

"This book," Elizabeth said, holding it out to her. "Can you tell us how much it costs?"

She held her breath as the woman leafed through it.

"Why, it's just an old textbook," the woman said. "I can let you have it for a dollar."

Amy let out a squeal and Julie clapped her hands. The woman looked at them in amused bewilderment. Quickly, Elizabeth explained their mission.

"What a marvelous idea," the woman commented.

"We're having a sixties dance, too," Julie told her. "Maybe we can find some clothes here to wear."

"I've got some more clothes in the back," the woman said. "Why don't you come back later this week and I'll show them to you?" Her twinkling eyes focused on George. "I may even have some old bell-bottom jeans for you."

George didn't say anything. He just reached in his pocket and pulled out a quarter. The girls each added a quarter, and the woman put the book in a paper bag.

"Where should we go next?" Elizabeth asked, clutching the bag tightly as they left the store.

"Let's go back to my place," Amy suggested. "We can ask my mother if she has any ideas."

"That's a good idea," Julie said. "It's not enough just to find things that are from the sixties. If we're going to win, we need to know what was special about the sixties."

Luckily, Amy's mother was happy to talk with them about the sixties. Over homemade cookies and milk, she shared her memories.

"It was an exciting time," she told them with a sentimental smile. "There were a lot of changes. Some were good. Some were terrible. I remember when President Kennedy was assassinated," Mrs. Sutton's face became somber. "That was a terrible time. In fact, I was just thinking about that the other day when I came across something. . . . " She got up and left the room. When she returned, she was carrying a photograph.

"It's President Kennedy," Elizabeth exclaimed. She recognized the photo from her history book. "And it's autographed!"

"I wrote him a letter when I was just about your age," Mrs. Sutton's smile returned. "And I got this."

The kids gazed at the photograph in awe. And then they looked at each other.

Amy said what they were all thinking. "This would be wonderful to put in the time capsule."

Mrs. Sutton looked thoughtful, and Elizabeth held her breath.

"Please Mom?" Amy pleaded.

Her mother nodded. "I think a time capsule is the perfect place for it. I'd like to know that twenty-five years from now, kids your age will still think about President Kennedy."

Amy threw her arms around her mother. "Now we've got two fantastic things. All we need is one more."

"But how are we ever going to find another item as terrific as the two we've got?" Julie asked.

"It's not going to be easy," Elizabeth said. "We've got to come up with some good ideas. I'll ask my parents, and Julie, you ask yours, and George—" she stopped suddenly, and blushed.

"I'll ask my aunt and uncle," George said.

"Fine," Elizabeth said quickly. "And we'll meet in class on Monday to compare ideas."

"*If* we have any," Amy said.

"Don't worry." Elizabeth spoke with more confidence than she actually felt. "We will!"

When Jessica got home that afternoon, a note on the refrigerator told her that her parents were out.

From upstairs, she could hear the muffled sound of music—that meant Steven was home, but his door was closed and he wouldn't hear her.

She crept lightly up the stairs and headed directly for Elizabeth's room. The door was open and the room was empty. She went inside and looked around.

This could be a waste of time, she thought. *Lizzie's team probably hasn't found anything yet. And even if they have, one of her teammates might be keeping the stuff.*

But she'd promised Lila she would look, and that's what she was here to do. Under the bed seemed like the logical place to start, so she knelt down and was just about to lift up the edge of the bedspread when she heard a voice.

"Jess! What are you doing?"

Jessica jumped up guiltily. "Oh! Uh, hi, Lizzie. I was just, uh, just looking for my—purple socks."

Elizabeth looked at her in puzzlement. "Under *my* bed?"

Jessica managed a weak smile. "Yeah, I thought maybe I took them off in here."

Elizabeth rolled her eyes and then grinned knowingly. "Tell the truth. You were trying to find out what my team has for the time capsule."

Jessica opened her eyes wide. "Oh, Lizzie," she said innocently, "you don't think I'd stoop that low, do you?"

Elizabeth laughed. "You can snoop all you want. We left our things at Amy's."

"Oh." So her team *had* found some items. She eyed her sister suspiciously. She was looking awfully pleased with herself. "How many things do you have?"

"Two," Elizabeth said happily. "And they're both pretty terrific."

Jessica sniffed. "Ha! I'll bet they're not as terrific as the stuff *we* found." She waited for Elizabeth to ask her what they were. But Elizabeth just smiled. "We'll see," was all she said.

"How's the contest going?" Steven was standing at the doorway, with his hands behind his back.

"My team's doing great," Jessica said quickly. "We've found two incredible things already."

"So has mine," Elizabeth added.

"But you need three, right?" Steven asked.

The girls nodded, and Steven grinned slyly. "Well, I just might have that third item right here." From behind his back, he brought forth a large book.

"What is it?" Jessica asked.

"A Sweet Valley Junior High yearbook. From the very first year the school opened."

Jessica let out a shriek. "Steven, that's fantastic! Give it to me!"

"Wait a minute," Elizabeth objected. "Why should he give it to you?"

"Because I asked for it first," Jessica replied. "C'mon, Steven, hand it over."

"Not so fast," Steven said. "I guess you could both use this, right?"

The girls nodded and Steven's grin broadened. "Then make me an offer."

Jessica thought rapidly. "I'll bake you a dozen brownies tonight. No, I'll bake two dozen. With nuts."

Steven turned to Elizabeth. "Care to top that?"

"I'll make your bed for the next two weeks," Elizabeth offered.

"Hey, that's not bad," Steven said thoughtfully.

"Wait," Jessica said frantically, "I'll make your bed for three weeks. *And* bake the brownies."

"Hmmm. This is getting better and better." He looked back at Elizabeth. "It's your turn."

Just then, Mrs. Wakefield appeared at the door. "Who's going to help me get dinner started?" Before any of them could speak, she noticed the book in Steven's hand. "What have you got there?"

With obvious reluctance, Steven handed it over.

"A Sweet Valley Junior High yearbook! Where did you find it?"

"It belongs to one of my friend's mothers," Steven muttered.

Jessica groaned silently. *So it wasn't even his to give away.* But she had to do something. She owed it to the Unicorns. "Steven," she wheedled, in her sweetest voice, "please, can I have it for the time capsule? My team only has two things, and we need one more. Pretty please."

"My team needs one more thing too," Elizabeth said firmly.

Mrs. Wakefield looked at Jessica, then at Elizabeth, and then at Steven. A slow smile spread across her face. "I think this yearbook is going right back to your friend's house. You have no right to auction off someone else's property. Besides, you'll make your sisters crazy."

Mrs. Wakefield closed the yearbook and tucked it under her arm. "Now let's all go and get dinner on the table." As she left the room, Jessica groaned. "Darn, I really wanted that yearbook."

"Me, too," Elizabeth sighed.

"Don't complain to me," Steven said. "*I* really wanted those brownies."

And in spite of everything, they all burst out laughing.

Four

◇

Elizabeth got to her social studies class early on Monday. Julie and Amy were already huddled with George at the back of the room. Elizabeth crossed her fingers and hoped that one of them had come up with a brilliant idea for the time capsule.

But as she approached, she could tell by their glum faces that no one had anything to offer. "I don't even know what to look for," Amy said mournfully.

"I saw this ad in a magazine," George remarked. "You can send away for a newspaper from any date."

"That's great, George. Maybe we can order one from an important date in the sixties," Julie proposed. Elizabeth and Amy looked at George hopefully.

"Yeah, except it costs twenty-five dollars," George informed them. Their faces fell. "And it takes three weeks to get it," he added. Their faces grew even longer. They had less than two weeks to come up with something fantastic.

But Elizabeth had a thought. "You know, they have old newspapers at the public library. Maybe if we looked at them we'd get some ideas for other items. Why don't we all go there after school today?"

Julie looked at her apologetically. "I can't. I've got a flute lesson."

"And I have to babysit," Amy said.

"I have to run an errand for my aunt," George said. "I'm sorry."

"That's OK," Elizabeth assured them. "We don't all have to do it. I'll go and I'll let you guys know tomorrow if I find anything."

All day at school, she heard rumors of the wonderful things other teams had found. It was hard to pay attention in class. Her mind kept wandering as she tried to think of something special her team could get. But it was no use. She could only hope she'd find the answer at the library. As soon as the final bell rang, Elizabeth ran out the doors and headed straight for the library.

Not wanting to waste any time, she went directly to the reference desk.

Mrs. Donaldson, the librarian, smiled at her. "Can I help you?"

"I want to look at some 1960s newspapers," Elizabeth told her.

"Come this way and I'll show you where they are," the librarian said. Elizabeth followed her to a room behind the reference desk.

There was a row of small desks, each with a screen. Elizabeth expected to see stacks and stacks of old yellowed newspapers. Instead, the room was lined with cabinets containing small boxes.

"What year would you like to look at first?" Mrs. Donaldson asked.

Elizabeth told her the year Sweet Valley Junior High first opened, and the librarian went to a cabinet. She took out one of the small boxes and handed it to Elizabeth. "Here you are."

Elizabeth stared at it blankly. Mrs. Donaldson must have noticed her bewildered expression, because she smiled kindly. "Have you ever used microfilm before?"

Elizabeth shook her head.

"We don't have the actual newspapers," the librarian explained. "The kind of paper used would disintegrate over time. And they would take up too much space. Instead, the newspapers are photographed on these rolls, and you use a microfilm reader to look at them. Do you know how to work this?"

With only a bit of instruction, Elizabeth learned how to operate the machine. In no time at all, she was exploring the pages, reading bits of stories and reports. It was amazing to read about events that had happened in Sweet Valley so long ago, long before she was even born.

Elizabeth found an article about the opening of Sweet Valley's brand-new junior high school, but decided a photocopied article just wouldn't be special enough.

After an hour, her eyes ached from staring at the screen. She'd gone through almost four months of newspapers and she still hadn't come up with any great ideas. She was just about ready to rewind the film when something caught her eye.

It was the sports page. And the headline read "Sweet Valley Wins State Junior High Football Championship." Entranced, Elizabeth began to read the article. *It must have been a thrilling game*, she thought. The score was tied until the last few minutes of the last quarter, when Sweet Valley got the ball, the quarterback threw it, and—

Elizabeth practically jumped out of her seat. She read the lines again and again to make sure her eyes weren't deceiving her. But there it was, in black and white.

" . . . and the winning touchdown was caught by Howard Henkel. The crowd went wild, and the team carried Henkel off the field on their shoulders. Later, Henkel was presented with the football as a memento of Sweet Valley Junior's first championship season."

Elizabeth fell back in her seat, amazed by her

discovery. Howard Henkel. That was Mr. Henkel, George's father. She was sure of that.

Mr. Henkel, that sad-looking man in a wheel-chair, had once led a football team to victory. How proud George must be!

And then she had a fantastic idea. What if Mr. Henkel still had that football? It would be the perfect addition to their collection. *Wait until the others heard about this!* Quickly, she rewound the film and replaced it in the box. She couldn't wait to get home and call Amy and Julie and George.

She was hurrying toward the exit when she was distracted by a book display. A sign over the books read NEW MYSTERIES. Elizabeth immediately thought of Mr. Henkel. She knew he liked mysteries so she picked out a couple and checked them out at the circulation desk. Then she practically flew all the way home.

When she arrived she ran upstairs, tossed her books on her bed, and went out to the phone in the hall. Rapidly, she dialed Amy's number.

"Did you find out anything at the library?" Amy asked.

"Did I! Wait till you hear!" Elizabeth told her about Mr. Henkel, and Amy got just as excited as she was.

"Do you think he kept the ball?" she asked.

"I'm going to call George right now and ask

him," Elizabeth said. "If his father has that ball, I'm sure he's shown it to George a million times."

"I'll call Julie and tell her the news," Amy said. "Elizabeth, if we get that football, we'll definitely win!"

"I know, I know," Elizabeth exclaimed. "I'll talk to you later." She hung up and looked for George's phone number in the Sweet Valley Middle School Directory.

A woman answered. "Hello?"

"May I speak to George, please? This is Elizabeth Wakefield."

A moment later, she heard George's soft voice. "Hi, Elizabeth."

"George, you won't believe what I found out at the library! Why didn't you tell us your father caught the winning touchdown pass at Sweet Valley Junior High? And they gave him the ball to keep! Does he still have it?"

There was a silence on the other end.

"George?"

Finally, he spoke. "I don't know what you're talking about."

"You didn't know your father was a football hero?" Elizabeth was bewildered. Wasn't that the kind of thing a father would share with his son?

"No."

And he didn't sound like he cared very much, either. Elizabeth didn't know what to say. She tried to collect her thoughts. "Well, could you ask him about the ball? If we could get it for the time capsule, George, we'd have the best three items."

Again, there was a silence before George spoke. And when he did, his voice was dull and lifeless. "No, I can't ask him."

He didn't offer any explanation and the tone in his voice told Elizabeth she shouldn't ask for one. But she couldn't help herself.

"Why not?"

"Because I never see my father," George replied flatly. "We don't even talk to each other."

Elizabeth was shocked. She'd never heard of such a thing—a father and his son not speaking?

But that's what George said. And that was all he was going to tell her. "Look, Elizabeth, I've got to go."

"But George," Elizabeth said in a rush, "he's your father! Why can't you—"

All she heard was a click on the other end of the line.

It took a moment for everything to sink in, then she hung up.

She went downstairs. Her father had just come home from work and he was sitting in the living room, reading the newspaper. He looked up as Elizabeth sat down next to him on the sofa.

"You look like you've got something on your mind."

"Dad, do you know Mr. Henkel very well?"

"Well, I wouldn't say we're close friends," Mr. Wakefield said. "But I've known him for quite a while."

"Was he always as quiet as he is now?" Elizabeth asked.

"Not at all," her father said. "In fact, he was a very likable guy and a terrific athlete. He planned to become a football coach."

"What happened? What made him change?"

Mr. Wakefield sighed. "He fought in Vietnam, and he was very badly wounded there. That's why he's in a wheelchair."

Elizabeth shuddered. "That's awful."

Her father nodded sadly. "And his wounds were more than physical. He came back a different man, bitter and angry at the world. His wife tried to help him, but he just wouldn't respond. Then she died when their son was still very young."

"George," Elizabeth murmured. "He's in my class at school."

"That's when his wife's sister took the baby," Mr. Wakefield continued.

"Dad, it's so tragic," Elizabeth cried. "They don't even speak to each other! I want to help them!"

Her father put his arm around her. "That's sweet of you, Elizabeth. And I know you mean well. But I really don't think there's anything any of us can do. You can be a friend to George, and you can be a friend to Mr. Henkel. But as far as their relationship goes, they'll have to work that out between themselves. Getting involved in other people's family problems isn't always a good idea."

"I know," Elizabeth said. "I should mind my own business."

"That's right."

Elizabeth wasn't even thinking about the football anymore. She was thinking about poor George. And poor Mr. Henkel. And even though she knew her father was right, she wished more than anything that there was something she could do to bring them together.

Five

◈

"He doesn't talk to his father at all?" Amy's expression was one of surprise.

"That's what he said," Elizabeth replied, keeping her voice low. They were standing outside their homeroom, and she didn't want anyone to overhear their conversation.

"Then I guess there's no chance we'll get that football," Amy said mournfully.

"I suppose not," Elizabeth said. "We don't even know if he still has it. When I asked George on the phone last night, he got so upset he hung up on me."

"You're kidding!" Amy's eyebrows shot up. "That doesn't sound like something George would do."

"Shh," Elizabeth cautioned her. She could see George coming toward them.

"I'll let you guys talk privately," Amy whispered, and hurried into the classroom. As George approached, Elizabeth gave him her brightest, warmest smile. He didn't smile back—but at least he didn't look angry.

And he got right to the point. "Look, Elizabeth, I'm sorry about last night. I shouldn't have yelled at you like that. And I shouldn't have hung up on you."

"That's OK," Elizabeth reassured him. "It was my fault. I shouldn't have pestered you like that."

George looked down at the floor. "It's just that I don't like to talk about my father."

"I understand," Elizabeth said. They stood there awkwardly, not even looking at each other. George wore the same dejected expression she'd seen so often on Mr. Henkel's face.

"George," Elizabeth said impulsively, "why don't you come to the dance Friday night?"

George grimaced. "I don't like dances. And I don't know the kids here at school that well."

"You know us," Elizabeth insisted. "You could go with me and Julie and Amy. It would be nice if we could all go together as a team."

George hesitated.

"Please? We'd really like you to be with us."

George looked surprised. "You would?"

"Absolutely," Elizabeth declared. "We'll have

fun! And maybe we could find out what some of the other kids are collecting for the time capsule. It might give us some fresh ideas."

She could tell that George was wavering. Finally, he gave her a half-smile and said, "OK."

"Oh, George, I'm so glad!" Elizabeth said happily. "Let's all go back to that little shop this week and see if we can find some clothes. And just think! You'll probably be the only boy at the dance with three dates!"

George blushed slightly, but his smile broadened. "I hope I can handle that!"

All that day, Elizabeth remembered George's smile, and she felt much better. Maybe there wasn't anything she could do about bringing George and his father back together, but at least she could help George feel better about himself.

When she got home from school that afternoon, her mother was going through the mail. "Oh, dear," Mrs. Wakefield remarked. "Here's something for Mr. Henkel that the mailman left in our box by mistake."

"I'll take it to him," Elizabeth offered. She took the letter from her mother and walked over to Mr. Henkel's house. Through a window, she could see him sitting in his chair, staring expressionlessly at a television. She rapped on the window and caught his attention.

Mr. Henkel looked up, and actually seemed pleased to see her. He beckoned for her to come in.

"Hi," Elizabeth greeted him. "What are you watching?"

"I don't know," Mr. Henkel said. "I'm not really watching it." He pointed to a book on his lap.

Elizabeth switched off the TV so she could hear herself talk. "I brought you a letter that was left in our mailbox."

"A letter?" Mr. Henkel asked in surprise. He took the envelope from Elizabeth. "Oh, it's just a bill."

He doesn't even get any personal letters, Elizabeth thought sympathetically. Then she thought about the boy described in the newspaper article, tearing across the football field. How could they be the same person?

Thinking of the newspaper article reminded her of something. "I got you some mystery books from the library," she told him. "But I left them at home. I can go back and get them now."

"Don't bother," Mr. Henkel said. "I'm in the middle of a mystery now."

"I'll bring them over on Saturday," Elizabeth promised.

"Thank you," Mr. Henkel said politely.

There didn't seem to be anything left to say. And yet, Elizabeth got the feeling he didn't really want her to leave. He must be so lonely, she thought. She should at least try to make some conversation with him.

"Speaking of the library," she said, "I saw your name there."

His brow wrinkled. "My name in the library?"

"I was looking at some newspapers from the sixties. You see, we're having a twenty-fifth anniversary celebration at school, and there's a contest to see who can bring in the best things from twenty-five years ago, when the school first opened. So I was going through these newspapers to get some ideas and I saw a story about you!"

A slow smile grew across Mr. Henkel's face. "The championship game," he murmured.

"That's right! The article said that you caught the winning touchdown pass."

His eyes misted over. "Yes, I did."

"Tell me about it," Elizabeth urged.

"Oh, I remember it well. We were a brand-new school, and we felt like we had something to prove. We didn't have a school song, or a mascot, or anything like that. But we knew how to play football, and we had a lot of spirit."

The book slid off his lap, but Mr. Henkel didn't even notice. He was completely caught up in his memories.

"The other team came from a school north of here. They'd been state champions for two years, and they were pretty sure of themselves. They thought they could just roll all over us." He laughed—not his usual bitter laugh, but a real laugh, a joyful one. "For a while, we thought they could, too! They had some really big guys on that team. But the coach gave us a great pep talk at halftime. He made us believe we could do anything. I remember thinking, I'm going to be a coach like that someday!"

Mr. Henkel began describing the play that won the game. Elizabeth didn't know too much about football, so she couldn't completely understand everything he was saying, but his description was so vivid, she almost felt like she was there. She could actually hear the roar of the crowd.

"A couple of guys hoisted me up and carried me on their shoulders back to the locker room. And boy, did we celebrate!"

Elizabeth laughed. "I'll bet you guys went crazy."

"We did," Mr. Henkel agreed, grinning. "Then the coach made a speech, telling us how proud he was. And he gave me something. Wait here. I'll show you."

He wheeled himself out of the room. Elizabeth held her breath. She had a pretty good idea what he was going to bring back.

Sure enough, he returned with a football in his lap. "This is the actual ball I caught in that game. Look, you can see where all the guys signed it."

Elizabeth carefully took the ball from him. The writing was faded, but the signatures were still visible.

"What a wonderful souvenir," she sighed. She debated asking the question that was on her mind. What harm would it do?

"This would be perfect for the contest," she began, but Mr. Henkel stopped her.

"I'm sorry, Elizabeth," he said, taking the ball back. "But I can't give you this. It's all I've got."

His voice had changed. His tone was cheerless and his usual melancholy expression had returned.

"I understand," Elizabeth said quickly. She got up. "I guess I'd better get home."

Mr. Henkel nodded. But his eyes remained glued to the ball he was clutching tightly.

"I'll be back soon with the library books," she called from the door.

How sad, she thought as she crossed the yard. His most precious possession is an old football. And he said it was all he had! What about his son? Wasn't a living person more important than a souvenir from twenty-five years ago?

At home, Jessica was sprawled in front of the television watching music videos. "Where have you been?" she asked Elizabeth.

"At Mr. Henkel's," Elizabeth told her.

Jessica made a face. "I don't see how you can stand that weird man."

Elizabeth was tempted to tell her that Mr. Henkel was once a football star, but she decided not to. If Jessica knew about the football he had, she just might go over there and pester him for it. "Have you collected all your things for the contest yet?"

"Maybe," Jessica said, grinning. "How about you?"

"We still need one more thing," Elizabeth said. "We're going crazy trying to think of something."

"Well, don't go too crazy," Jessica warned her. "I mean, it's not as if you could actually win."

"Why not?"

"Because if you could see what we've got already, you'd know your team doesn't stand a chance!"

Elizabeth laughed. "We'll see about that!" And she went upstairs to use the phone.

"Amy? Hi, it's Elizabeth. Guess what? Mr. Henkel *does* have the football."

"Oh, wow!" Amy squealed.

"Don't get excited," Elizabeth said. "I asked him, and he won't let us have it."

"Darn," Amy groaned. "Did you tell him George was on our team?"

"No. Why?"

"I was just thinking," Amy said slowly. "Maybe if he knew George wanted it, he'd give it to him."

"I don't think we could get George to ask him," Elizabeth said. "I told you how he acted when I mentioned his father."

"I know," Amy sighed. "It was just an idea."

"But I did talk George into going to the dance with us Friday night," Elizabeth added.

"You did? That's great! He's really a nice guy, Elizabeth. Maybe going to the dance will cheer him up."

"Maybe," Elizabeth agreed. "But I think it's going to take a lot more than a dance to make George really happy."

"Yeah," Amy said. " I know what you mean."

After she hung up, Elizabeth went to her room to start on her homework. But she found it hard to concentrate. She just kept thinking about George and the football.

Maybe Amy was right. Maybe they *should* try to talk George into asking his father for the ball.

Elizabeth had a feeling that ball could be more than just a winning item. It could be the one thing that might bring a father and son back together.

Six

◇

On Friday afternoon, Jessica went into the kitchen clutching a battered magazine. "Mom, where's the ironing board?"

Her mother looked at her in astonishment, and Jessica couldn't blame her. Ironing was not known to be one of Jessica's favorite activities.

"Why, it's where it always is, honey, downstairs, in the laundry room," Mrs. Wakefield told her. "Are you ironing your things for tonight's dance?"

"Uh, yes," Jessica replied. *That wasn't really a lie,* she thought. She *was* planning to iron something for tonight. But it wasn't her clothes.

She ran downstairs to the laundry room and closed the door. Then she plugged in the iron and set it at its lowest setting. She waited a moment for the iron to heat up and then she bent down and spread her hair over the ironing board.

Behind her, the door opened.

"Jessica! What are you doing?"

Jessica raised her head and grinned at her sister. "I'm ironing my hair."

Elizabeth's mouth fell open. "What are you doing *that* for? Your hair's already straight!"

"It's not straight *enough*. Wait, I'll show you." Jessica opened her magazine and pointed to a picture. "Look at that girl." The model in the picture had long, completely straight hair, without even the slightest hint of a wave.

"I found this fashion magazine from the sixties," Jessica went on. "*All* the girls in it have their hair like this. That's how I want to look tonight. Tamara's mother told us she used to iron her hair to get it like this. So I want to try it."

Elizabeth shuddered. "If you ask me, it sounds kind of dangerous. Does Mom know you're doing this?"

"No! And you'd better not tell her, either."

Elizabeth didn't need to. At that very minute, Mrs. Wakefield appeared at the door, holding a can.

"Do you need some spray starch?" she asked Jessica.

Jessica pictured what her hair would look like if she starched it—sticking straight out like a petticoat. "No, thanks, Mom."

Mrs. Wakefield glanced around curiously. "Where are your clothes?"

Jessica tugged on a lock of her hair. "Uh, I was just going to get them."

Her mother eyed her suspiciously. "Jessica, what are you up to?"

Elizabeth started to giggle, and Jessica shot a furious look at her. Then she gave up, knowing that her mother would find out anyway. "I'm going to iron my hair so it's perfectly straight. You know, the way everyone had their hair in the sixties."

Mrs. Wakefield strode over to the iron and unplugged it. "Oh, no, you're not. Do you have any idea how dangerous this could be?"

"Mom!" Jessica wailed, but Mrs. Wakefield just shook her head.

"You know, I had a friend who used to do that when we were in high school. One day she lifted the iron, and half her hair came off."

"But I want to look like that," Jessica whined, pointing to the photo in the magazine. Her mother studied the picture.

"There are other ways to get your hair straight like that," Mrs. Wakefield said. "If you'd like, I'll show you how."

"I thought girls snarled their hair into big puffy styles in the sixties," Elizabeth said.

"That was in the early sixties," her mother told her. "Would you like to wear your hair like that?"

"You really should try that," Jessica said eagerly. "It sounds wonderful." In all honesty, she thought it sounded awful, but she didn't want Elizabeth looking the same way she did at the dance.

Elizabeth looked doubtful, but she nodded bravely. "Well, OK, I'll try it."

"Both of you, go wash your hair, and let me know when you're ready." Mrs. Wakefield left the room, and Elizabeth began flipping through the pages of Jessica's magazine.

"Where did you find this?" she asked. "Are you going to submit it for the time capsule?"

Jessica snatched it back. "Maybe." Actually, her team was only holding on to the magazine as a last resort. But she gave Elizabeth her haughtiest look. "Now I guess *you're* going to start running around looking for an old magazine."

Elizabeth smiled in a way that made Jessica uncomfortable. "No, we're working on getting something much more exciting than an old magazine." With that, she sailed out of the laundry room.

Jessica stared after her glumly. She was probably bluffing, but what if she really did have something wonderful? She'd find out one way or another, but right now she had other things on her mind. Like her hair.

A half hour later, she was sitting on a chair in her room while her mother brushed out her long blond locks. "This is how I did it when I was your age," Mrs. Wakefield said. "To get my hair really straight, I used to wrap it. I'd wind a lock around my head, and secure it tightly with clips."

"Ouch!" Jessica cried out as a clip dug into her scalp.

"Sorry," her mother said with a grin, "but it sometimes takes pain to be beautiful."

Jessica gritted her teeth as her mother wound the locks of hair tighter and tighter. "Boy, I'm glad I wasn't a teenager in your day," she complained. "I wouldn't want to go through this every day."

Mrs. Wakefield smiled. "Wait till you see what I do to Elizabeth."

"I hope she has to suffer as much as I'm suffering," Jessica muttered.

"All done," her mother declared. "Now you've got to let it dry, and I'll go start on Elizabeth."

Jessica followed her to Elizabeth's room. Elizabeth sat at her desk, looking apprehensively at a pile of big curlers stuffed with bristles.

Deftly, Mrs. Wakefield went to work, winding Elizabeth's hair on curlers and sticking in bobby pins. Elizabeth winced as the bristles hit her scalp.

"Would you believe I used to sleep on these things almost every night?" her mother asked.

"That must have been painful," Elizabeth sympathized.

"It was," Mrs. Wakefield agreed. "You girls are very lucky that the natural look is in style now."

Jessica started laughing. "You look like a creature from outer space."

Elizabeth looked at her reflection in the mirror, and she had to agree. The curlers made her head look twice its size.

Then Jessica looked at her reflection glumly. At least Elizabeth looked worse than she did.

The minute the twins walked into the dining room, Steven took one look at them and ducked under the table. "Help! We're being invaded by creatures from another planet!"

Mr. Wakefield glanced at the twins and practically jumped. "Oh no! Not again. I thought those days were gone," he declared.

"It's for the sixties dance tonight," Jessica informed him.

"Oh, that's right," her father said. "And how are your time capsule projects coming along?"

"My team's got two terrific things already," Elizabeth announced. "All we need is one more. And if we can get what we think we might get, we'll be a shoo-in."

Jessica glared at her. Then she beamed at her father. "My team's got great things, too."

"That's good," Mr. Wakefield said. "I'm glad to see this isn't turning into a battle between the two of you."

"Oh, no," Elizabeth said. "Nothing like that."

"There's no battle," Jessica echoed, looking at her sister. *Not yet,* she thought.

"Wow!" Elizabeth exclaimed as she entered the gym with Julie, Amy, and George. "This is cool!"

The gym was decorated with streamers and balloons. All over the walls were posters of rock groups and movie stars who were popular in the 1960s. At one end of the room, a disc jockey was playing records Elizabeth had heard on the local radio's oldies station. At the other end was a long table covered with refreshments.

And the kids looked wild. "Look at Bruce Patman," Amy squealed. Bruce was wearing a white guru shirt, blue bell-bottom pants, and a peace medallion around his neck. Another boy was wearing a long-haired wig.

Elizabeth adjusted her pale yellow shirtwaist dress. She'd found it at the junk shop, and her mother had assured her she had one almost exactly like it when she was Elizabeth's age. Then she touched her hair. It felt totally unfamiliar, all teased up in a big bouffant hairdo and stiff with hairspray.

Across the room she spotted Jessica with Lila and the other Unicorns. They were all wearing purple miniskirts but Jessica looked the best. She had added a pair of white patent leather go-go boots to her outfit. And her hair was absolutely straight, just like her mother had promised it would be.

"I'm going to get something to eat," Julie announced.

George looked around uneasily, and played with his wide, flowered tie. "I'll come with you," he said, and the two of them headed toward the refreshments.

"Are you going to ask George about the football?" Amy asked Elizabeth.

"Maybe later," Elizabeth said. "Let's get something to drink." They went over to the refreshment table to join Julie and George, who were watching the other kids dance. Then Ms. Luster, the librarian from school, joined them.

"Why aren't you kids dancing?" Ms. Luster asked, her bright eyes twinkling.

"I've never danced to this kind of music," Elizabeth confessed. She had a feeling most of the others hadn't either. The few who were actually on the dance floor were looking pretty awkward.

The disc jockey put on a new record. "That's a twist record!" Ms. Luster exclaimed. "Now, I know you can do that. It's very easy. Watch me!"

She pulled them out to the dance floor and gave a little demonstration. All four of them stared at each other in amazement. The librarian was twisting from the waist, back and forth, to the beat of the music.

"Awesome!" George declared.

Ms. Luster laughed. "We would have said 'far out'! Here, I'll show you how to do it. Bend your knees a little, put your arms out like this, and just go!"

By now, a small crowd had gathered around the librarian, and everyone was trying it. "Very good!" Ms. Luster declared. "Excellent, George! You're better than Chubby Checker!"

"Who's Chubby Checker?" Amy whispered to Elizabeth.

"I don't know," Elizabeth replied. "I guess he was a famous twister."

"This is a good dance to do when you're shy," Ms. Luster told them. "Because you don't even have to hold hands with your partner."

George turned a little red. "No wonder I'm so good at it," he told Elizabeth.

Elizabeth laughed. She had never heard George make a joke before!

"Look, Nora Mercandy just came in," Julie said.

Elizabeth waved to her. Nora looked great. She was dressed like a hippie, with a short, embroidered dress and strands of beads around her neck.

Then she noticed George was looking at Nora, too, and he was getting redder. He likes her, Elizabeth thought.

"George, why don't you ask Nora to dance?" Elizabeth suggested.

George was blushing furiously: "She might not know how to do this twist thing."

"Then you can show her!" Julie said. George bit his lip.

"Oh, go on and do it," Elizabeth urged.

"OK," George said. And with his face set determinedly, he started toward Nora. A few seconds later, they were on the dance floor.

She watched George and Nora for a few moments and then went back to dancing with her friends.

Every time Elizabeth saw George for the rest of the night, she could tell he was having a great time. He was dancing a lot, and talking to kids he had never spoken to before.

Since he was in such a good mood, Elizabeth decided she would ask him about the football. But it had to be at exactly the right moment.

It came when they were getting ready to leave. She and George were waiting for Julie and Amy outside the gym door, where Julie's father was going to pick them up.

"George," she said slowly, "remember when I told you about your father winning the football championship?"

She watched his expression carefully. He didn't freeze up like he had the last time she mentioned his father. He just nodded.

"Well, I was over at your father's a few days ago, and he showed me the football. I asked him if we could have it for our contest, but he said no."

"That's too bad," George said. "It would have been perfect."

"We were thinking," Elizabeth continued, "that maybe you could ask him for it. I mean, since you're his son, he just might let you have it."

She held her breath. Would George even consider doing this? It would mean he'd have to see his father, talk to him. But maybe, just maybe, this could start off a whole new relationship for them.

George was silent for a few minutes. He seemed to be thinking very hard. Then he smiled. "OK. I'll ask him."

Elizabeth wanted to jump for joy!

Seven

◇

The next morning, Elizabeth hummed a Beatles song as she fixed herself some breakfast. When her father walked in, she greeted him cheerfully.

"Good morning," she sang out. "Isn't it a beautiful day?"

She giggled at her father's expression as he looked out the window and saw all the clouds.

"I guess I just feel so good that it seems like a beautiful day," Elizabeth explained.

"I suppose this means you had a good time at the dance last night," her father remarked as he poured himself a cup of coffee.

"I did," Elizabeth said, sitting down at the kitchen table with her grapefruit. "But it was even better watching George Henkel have such a good time."

Mr. Wakefield joined her at the table. "And I'm

guessing from that pleased expression on your face that you had something to do with that."

In all modesty, Elizabeth had to admit she deserved a little credit. "You know, Dad, he's always been so quiet, no one ever knew who he was!" She bit into a section of her grapefruit and chewed thoughtfully.

"He wasn't even planning to go to the dance," she went on. "But I knew if he just relaxed and opened up to people, he'd have a good time. And I was right!"

"Good for you," her father declared. "That's a nice feeling, to know you've helped someone."

"And there's more," Elizabeth continued. "I think I've come up with a way to get George and his father together."

Mr. Wakefield's smile faded a little. "Now, Elizabeth, remember what I told you about getting involved in a family's problems. That's a very private business. And sometimes an outsider can do more harm than good." His expression was serious.

But Elizabeth wasn't discouraged. "It'll be OK," she assured him. "I just have a feeling everything's going to work out perfectly." She just hoped George wouldn't change his mind about going to see his father.

A little while later, Elizabeth was up in her room doing her homework. When she gazed out the window, she noticed George Henkel walking up the street past her house. *Where is he going?* She asked herself.

She squinted as his figure grew smaller. And then she almost bit the eraser off the pencil that she had pressed to her mouth. He turned onto the block where his father lived.

Elizabeth hugged herself in glee. It was actually happening! Everything was going to be OK. She couldn't concentrate on her math problems as she tried to imagine exactly what was going on in Mr. Henkel's house. She pictured George and his father hugging, making up over whatever it was that had kept them apart for so long. Maybe they'd start doing things together, like going to football games . . . Maybe right this minute Mr. Henkel was handing George the famous football for the time capsule project. They'd win the contest and get their pictures placed in the capsule. And twenty-five years from now, people would know who they were.

She was so caught up in her fantasies that she was only vaguely aware of the doorbell ringing downstairs.

"I'll get it," she heard her brother call out. A moment later Steven was standing in her doorway. "You'd better fix your hair. It's a *boy*."

Who could it be, Elizabeth wondered. She took a quick look in the mirror, and groaned. Her hair was still matted from the night before. She grabbed a brush and yanked it through her hair. It wasn't much improvement. Quickly, she pulled it back in a ponytail, and ran downstairs.

George Henkel stood awkwardly in the middle of the living room. Elizabeth took one look at his face, and her heart sank.

"George! What's the matter?"

"I went to see my father," he said woodenly. "Big mistake."

Elizabeth motioned for him to come sit on the couch with her.

"Oh, George," was all she could think to say.

"I asked him about the football." He looked up, and Elizabeth could see the pain in his eyes. "He said there was no way he'd give me the most important thing in his life."

Elizabeth gasped. How could Mr. Henkel talk like that to his own son?

"What's the matter with him?" she cried out.

George jumped to his feet. "He doesn't care about me," he said passionately. "He's a hateful person who just wants to sit around and feel sorry for himself!" For a moment George looked like he was going to explode. His face was red and his fists were clenched.

"Look, Elizabeth," he said flatly. "I'm sorry about the football. I guess we'll just have to come up with something else. I'll see you at school." With that, he walked out.

Elizabeth sat there, staring into space. Ten minutes earlier she had felt wonderful. Now she was miserable. And it wasn't because of the football. George was even sadder than he'd been before. And it was all her fault.

Jessica lay on her bed and stared up at the ceiling. Her team still hadn't found a third great item for the contest, and there was only a week left. Of course, they had that fashion magazine, but she knew that wouldn't impress the judges. They needed something big, something as important as the poster and the record album.

She went out into the hallway and dialed Lila's number. "Have you thought of anything?" she asked when Lila answered.

"No," Lila replied. "What about you?"

"Nothing," Jessica said mournfully. "I found out what Elizabeth's team has, though. I overheard her and Amy talking at the dance."

"Oh, really?" Lila's voice perked up. "What have they got?"

Jessica sneered. "Really dumb stuff. Some book and a picture of President Kennedy."

"Oh, well," Lila said in relief, "at least we've got better stuff than that."

"But I know they're working on getting something big," Jessica went on. "I just don't know what it is."

"Well, find out," Lila insisted. "And then

maybe we can get it before they do. Whatever it is."

"I will," Jessica promised. She hung up the phone, and went to Elizabeth's room. The door was slightly ajar, and she pushed it open.

Elizabeth was in the same position Jessica had been in moments before—lying on her bed, staring at the ceiling. But she looked even more depressed.

Her expression gave Jessica hope. Elizabeth obviously hadn't gotten her hands on whatever it was she was after for the time capsule contest.

"Don't you have a riding class today?" Jessica asked.

Elizabeth glanced at the clock on her nightstand, and leaped off the bed. "Oh my gosh, I'm late!" She dashed to her dresser, pulled out her riding clothes, and got her boots from the closet. Just as she was changing her clothes, something caught her eye.

"Oh no," she moaned. "I forgot to drop those library books at Mr. Henkel's and I promised I'd bring them today. Jessica, could you take them over to him for me?"

"Are you kidding?" Jessica yelped. "That man gives me the creeps. Take them over yourself."

"I don't have time," Elizabeth wailed. "*Please*, Jessica?"

Jessica was about to refuse again when Elizabeth grabbed a bracelet from her dresser. "I'll let you wear this," she said.

Jessica hesitated. She had been admiring Elizabeth's new bracelet. It would look absolutely perfect with the outfit she was planning to wear to school on Monday.

"OK," she relented. "I'll take the books."

Elizabeth flashed her a grateful smile. "Thanks, Jess." And she ran out of the room.

Jessica eyed the books distastefully. Well, she might as well get this over with. She grabbed the books and headed over to Mr. Henkel's.

When he opened the door, Jessica was surprised to see that he was smiling. Every time she'd seen him before, he looked mean.

"Hi," he said, "come on in."

Hesitantly, Jessica entered the house. "I brought these books," she began, but Mr. Henkel wasn't listening.

"I'm glad you're here, Elizabeth," Mr. Henkel said. "I wanted to talk to you."

Jessica was about to tell him she wasn't Elizabeth, but Mr. Henkel wouldn't let her get a word in. "I've changed my mind," he said. "I want to give you the football."

Jessica stared at him in bewilderment. What was he talking about? What football?

"I'm ashamed about the way I treated George this morning," he went on. "And I want to make it up to him. I don't know how I could have believed a football meant more to me than my own son."

Jessica shifted the library books to her other arm and gazed at the man uneasily. "Uh, Mr. Henkel, I think you made a mistake. I'm— "

"I know I made a mistake," Mr. Henkel interrupted her. "I just hope it's not too late to correct it. Wait here."

He wheeled himself out of the room. Jessica put the books on a table and debated running out of the house. But before she could decide, Mr. Henkel reappeared, clutching a football.

He held it out toward Jessica. Gingerly, she took it from him. It didn't look very clean.

"You know," Mr. Henkel mused, "I look back on that moment twenty-five years ago when I caught the pass and won the championship for Sweet Valley Junior High, and it seems like the happiest moment in my life. I wonder if I can ever be that happy again. That's why the football means so much to me."

He paused and sighed deeply. "But my own son means more to me, even if I can't show him my real feelings. So I want you to give him the football."

Slowly, the meaning of what he was saying came to her. It was all starting to make sense. George Henkel was on Elizabeth's team. This football came from a championship game twenty-five years ago. This was what Elizabeth's team had been desperately trying to get.

"I do love my son," Mr. Henkel was saying. "I

just can't seem to tell him that. Maybe this football can say it for me."

But Jessica wasn't listening. All she could think about was the football. With this old piece of leather, there was no doubt about it. Her team would win!

Eight

◇

Jessica was in a great mood when she jumped out of bed Monday morning. She dressed quickly and then began rummaging through her closet. She knew that somewhere there was an old tote bag big enough to hold—and hide—a football.

All she had to do was get the football to school, where she could hide it in her locker. After throwing a number of items out of her closet, she finally found the old tote bag. She tossed the ball in, hoisted the bag over her shoulder, and started to leave the room. Then she caught a glimpse of herself in the mirror and she groaned.

The bag was made of thin nylon and the outline of the ball was very clear. Anyone would be able to see that she was carrying a football—including Elizabeth.

She *could* try to get out of the house before Elizabeth saw her, but that was too much of a risk. And then came a rap on her bedroom door.

"Jess? Are you ready for breakfast?" Elizabeth called.

"Just a minute," Jessica called out. Frantically, her eyes swept the room. How could she hide the football?

In desperation, she opened a dresser drawer and began pulling out her heaviest sweaters. She stuffed them in the bag, around the football. Then she lifted it over her shoulder, and checked her reflection in the mirror.

It was big and heavy and bulky, and it would be a real drag carrying it to school. But at least no one would be able to tell what was inside.

With the tote bag over one arm and her schoolbooks cradled in the other, she went downstairs. She debated leaving the bag by the front door, but she didn't want to let it out of her sight. Keeping her arm clenched around it tightly, she went into the kitchen.

"What would you like for breakfast?" her mother asked.

"Nothing, thanks," Jessica replied. "I have to get to school early."

Elizabeth eyed her curiously as she buttered a slice of toast. Jessica wasn't surprised by her expression. Rushing off to school was not something she did regularly.

"If you wait one minute, I'll walk with you,"

Elizabeth offered, biting her toast. "You look like you could use some help carrying all that stuff."

"I can't wait," Jessica said. "I'm in a rush." Even though the sweaters hid the shape of the ball, she felt nervous having Elizabeth looking at the bag. And she certainly didn't want her carrying it.

"What are you carrying in that bag?" Mrs. Wakefield asked.

Jessica tried to sound casual. "Just some stuff for a school project."

Elizabeth smiled a little wistfully. "I'll bet you have something for the contest in there." Then she sighed. "I was hoping my team was going to have something really terrific, but it didn't work out."

Somehow, Jessica managed to keep a straight face. "Gee, that's too bad. Well, I'll see you later. Bye, Mom." And she dashed out.

When she got to school, she spotted Lila and Tamara in the hallway outside their homeroom, and ran up to them. "Wait till you see what I've got," Jessica crowed. She couldn't wait to see their faces when she opened the bag. "Right here, in this tote bag, is something from the sixties that's going to win this contest for us."

"Did you find out what Elizabeth's team was after?" Lila asked.

Jessica nodded proudly. "And I got it first."

Tamara peered into the bag. "What is it—a sweater?"

"No, dummy, it's under the sweater." Jessica motioned for them to move in closer. "I don't want anyone else to know about this." She pulled out the top sweater, revealing what lay underneath.

Lila gazed at it doubtfully. "A football? What's so great about an old football?"

"It's not just any old football," Jessica announced. "This is the football that was used in the first championship game at Sweet Valley Junior High."

She was pleased to see how impressed the others looked. In fact, they were more than impressed. They were ecstatic.

"Jessica, that's fantastic!" Lila exclaimed. "Where did you find it?"

Jessica giggled. "It belongs to this man who lives near me. He thought he was giving it to Elizabeth and I just let him believe I was her!"

"Wow," Lila said in awe, "that was brilliant." Tamara agreed enthusiastically.

Jessica basked in their admiration. "We better go put it in my locker with the other things." The girls hurried down the hall, meeting Ellen Riteman and Betsy Gordon along the way. They showed them the football and they were suitably impressed.

"Jessica, the Unicorns are going to love you," Ellen pronounced. And Jessica beamed.

They gathered around her locker while Jessica dialed the combination and opened it. Then she held the bag open while Tamara pulled the football out.

"Hey, what are you girls doing with that football?"

Jessica turned to see Bruce Patman standing there, watching them. She smiled pertly.

"None of your business," she said while the other girls giggled. She wasn't worried. Bruce would never figure out where the ball came from.

What worried Jessica was that Caroline Pearce had overheard their conversation about the football. She was the school gossip and she could never keep her mouth shut when she had interesting news.

But surely Caroline must realize how important it was to keep this quiet, she thought to herself. And she shut the locker.

Elizabeth left her social studies class feeling like a cloud of gloom was hanging over her head. No one else on her team had come up with anything for the time capsule. And George had looked even more dejected than ever.

As she walked down the hall toward her next class, Nora Mercandy came running up to her. Nora didn't look particularly happy, either. Her usually lively eyes were dark with concern.

"What's the matter?" Elizabeth asked.

"It's George Henkel," Nora said, frowning. "I tried to talk to him this morning, and he was really unfriendly. Honestly, Elizabeth, I don't understand him. I thought he liked me at the dance Friday night. Today he won't even look at me."

"I think he's got something on his mind," Elizabeth said vaguely. "Don't take it too personally." She didn't want to tell Nora the whole story.

"Well, I wish he had *me* on his mind," Nora murmured. "He's on your time capsule team, isn't he?"

Elizabeth nodded. "Are you on a team, too?"

"No," Nora said. "I didn't have time to start running around looking for things. Did you guys come up with some good stuff?"

"We've got two things," Elizabeth told her. "We haven't been able to find a third item, though."

"Your sister's team is doing great," Nora remarked. "I don't know what else she's got, but I heard about the football. That's really neat."

Elizabeth stopped suddenly. "What football?"

Nora's eyes widened. "Haven't you heard? Caroline Pearce told me, and I figured everyone must know by now."

"Know *what*?"

"Jessica has the football that was used in Sweet Valley Junior High's first championship game. The man who caught the winning pass gave it to her."

It took a moment for the words to sink in. And when they did, Elizabeth was stunned. She couldn't believe what she was hearing. "Nora, are you sure?"

Nora shrugged. "That's what Caroline told me."

For a second, Elizabeth felt dizzy from the shock. Then she told Nora she had to get to class and ran off. She needed some time alone to absorb this news and think it through.

It just doesn't make sense, Elizabeth thought. *Mr. Henkel told George the ball was the most important thing in the world to him. Why did he suddenly decide to give it away like that? And why would he give the ball to Jessica, whom he hardly knew, instead of his very own son?*

No, nothing was making sense. Something very strange was going on. And Elizabeth was pretty sure she knew exactly what it was.

Sitting at a table in the cafeteria, Jessica felt like a queen at a banquet. Word of the famous football had spread rapidly among the Unicorns, and everyone came by the table to congratulate her. Even Janet Howell, Lila's cousin and president of the Unicorns, left her table of eighth-graders and made a special trip to Jessica's table.

"The Unicorns are very happy about this," she told Jessica. "This is a great accomplishment and we won't forget it."

Jessica smiled at Janet's praise as Lila watched her through narrowed eyes.

"Don't forget," she noted, "*I* was the one who got us the poster. And *that's* an important item, too."

"Of course it is," Janet assured her. "But the football is even better."

Lila scowled. Jessica could tell she felt jealous. And that made her feel great. She loved being envied—particularly by someone like Lila. She was on top of the world.

"Uh, oh, here comes Elizabeth," Tamara muttered.

Sure enough, there was her sister, striding across the cafeteria toward them. And she looked *mad*.

She found out about the ball, Jessica thought, and a knot suddenly formed in her stomach.

But what could Elizabeth do about it, anyway? The ball was in Jessica's locker. And that's where it would stay. Jessica geared herself for the confrontation.

Elizabeth came up beside her and blurted out. "How did you get that football?"

Jessica was aware of the other Unicorns watching and listening. She stood up so she and Elizabeth would be eye to eye.

"I didn't steal it, if that's what you're thinking. Mr. Henkel gave it to me."

"That doesn't make sense," Elizabeth snapped. "He barely knows you. Why would he give you that football?"

Jessica shrugged innocently. "I have no idea. But when I went over there Saturday to drop off the library books, he gave it to me."

Elizabeth glared at her suspiciously. "He didn't by any chance call you Elizabeth, did he?"

Jessica faltered. "Why would he do that?"

"Because he thought you were me. And that's why he gave you the ball."

"He wasn't planning to give it to *you*," Jessica snapped. "It was George—" she stopped herself, but it was too late. Elizabeth's eyes were gleaming.

"That's just what I thought," Elizabeth declared in triumph. "He wanted George to have the ball. And he gave it to you because he thought you were me. And he wanted me to give it to George. Right?"

Jessica wasn't about to admit to anything. "You're just jealous because we've got the ball," she said.

"Oh, really?" Elizabeth smiled grimly. "I guess I'll just have to go call Mr. Henkel and ask him who he thinks he gave the ball to."

"That's blackmail!" Tamara declared.

Elizabeth didn't respond. She just stood there, looking at Jessica evenly.

Jessica knew it was all over. If Elizabeth called Mr. Henkel, she'd find out the truth. And Mr. Henkel might call her parents about it, and tell them Jessica took the ball under false pretenses. She could be in serious trouble. There was no way out.

"Where's the ball?" Elizabeth asked quietly.

"In my locker," Jessica muttered.

"Then let's go get it. Right now."

Jessica could barely bring herself to look at the Unicorns. Just a minute ago, she'd been the most popular member. Now they would all be furious with her. She gave them a helpless look and an apologetic shrug. Then she followed Elizabeth out of the cafeteria.

Clutching the ball tightly, Elizabeth waited outside the door at school. She knew George had to come out this way. She couldn't wait to show him the ball and tell him his father wanted him to have it. He would be thrilled!

Finally, she spotted him walking slowly toward the exit doors. She edged through the crowd of departing students to reach him. "George! Look!"

George stared at the football. "Where did you get that?"

Quickly, Elizabeth explained what happened. "I finally got Jessica to confess that your father told her to give it to you. He's changed his mind, George! He wants you to have it!"

She waited for a big smile to break out on his face. But it didn't appear. George just kept staring at the ball. And his eyes were cold.

"So he wants me to have it. Well, maybe I don't want it anymore."

Elizabeth was startled. "George, what are you talking about? Think of the time capsule! And think about your father! If he wants you to have this, it's because he loves you."

George snorted. "If he loves me so much, he can see me face to face and give it to me himself. Otherwise, I don't want it. And you can tell him that." Without another word, he walked away.

For the second time that day, Elizabeth was in a state of shock. She shook her head in disbelief. She realized she had to go right over to Mr. Henkel's to relay George's message. All Mr. Henkel had to do was ask George to come over and present the ball to him. Surely he could do that. It would solve everything. George would know his father loved him and their team would win the contest. There was still hope!

Elizabeth ran all the way home. She knew she looked pretty silly running with the ball tucked under her arm. And sure enough, when she passed Bruce Patman and some of his buddies, Bruce yelled out, "Hey, somebody tackle her!"

Luckily, nobody did. Elizabeth ignored them and kept on running. By the time she reached her block, she was out of breath. She didn't even bother to stop at her own house, but headed directly to Mr. Henkel's.

"Elizabeth! It's good to see you!" Mr. Henkel said with a smile when he opened the door. But he looked puzzled when he noticed the football. "Didn't you give it to George like I asked you to?"

Elizabeth didn't tell him about Jessica's scheme. "I tried to," she told Mr. Henkel. "But George said he won't accept it unless you give it to him personally. I thought maybe you could call him now, and—" Her voice trailed off as she saw the man's expression change. He looked cold, angry, and bitter.

"I see," he said harshly. "He wants me to apologize and ask his forgiveness, is that it?"

"Oh, no!" Elizabeth cried out. "That's not it at all! He only wants—"

"I know what he wants," Mr. Henkel barked. "I can see he wants me to beg him to accept this. And I guess he doesn't realize that I'm unable to get down on my hands and knees."

"Mr. Henkel, please listen to me," Elizabeth pleaded, but it was no use.

"You tell my son that if he doesn't want my football, that's fine with me. Goodbye, Elizabeth."

And he closed the door.

Nine

◇

Jessica was in disgrace. She had let the Unicorns down. She kept telling them that there was nothing she could do about it. If her parents found out how she had gotten that football, she could have been grounded for life!

But her teammates weren't very sympathetic. Both Tamara and Ellen believed she should have risked getting into trouble and kept the ball.

"A Unicorn stops at nothing to win," Ellen kept reminding her.

"You were only looking out for yourself," Tamara said. "A Unicorn should think about what's good for the group."

"It wouldn't be good for the Unicorns if *I* got into trouble," Jessica shot back. "Can you imagine what people would say about us if they knew I had fooled Mr. Henkel into giving me that football?"

That shut them up a little. And Janet Howell, who had witnessed the scene between Jessica and Elizabeth, stood up for Jessica.

"Jessica's right," she told the others. "She did the only thing she could do under the circumstances. It may not matter to us how she got the football, but other people might not understand. And if they found out, it could hurt our reputation."

Jessica was relieved to have the Unicorn president on her side. She knew that eventually the rest of the members would forget about it.

The team gathered in Jessica's bedroom after school that day. Ellen, Tamara, and Betsy were still a little angry at her. And, as Jessica suspected, Lila used the situation to her advantage. Even though she wouldn't show it, Jessica knew Lila was actually pleased that she had lost the football. It put her in a superior position again.

"Thank goodness we still have the poster *I* bought," Lila told them. "And the record album we found in *my* house. Otherwise we wouldn't have a chance."

"But what are we going to do for a third item?" Tamara whined. "We need three to win."

"We'll use the fashion magazine," Lila stated. "It's not great, but the other two things are so fantastic they'll make up for it."

"It's certainly a better collection than my sister's

team has," Jessica piped up. "I mean, who cares about an old book and a dumb photograph?"

"But now she's got the football," Ellen reminded her, as if Jessica needed reminding. "That's going to make a big difference."

Jessica tried to sound more confident than she felt when she said, "Not big enough. Not when her other two things are so stupid." She looked at Lila hopefully.

Lila raised her eyebrows and scowled for a second, but then she nodded. "That's probably true. And I've heard about some of the stuff the other teams have, and they're no better. I think we've still got a good chance at winning."

The others all agreed.

"Of course," Lila added, giving Jessica a disapproving look, "we would have had a better chance with the football."

Jessica wanted to change the subject. "I'll go get us some sodas," she declared, jumping up. She knew the minute she left the room, they'd all start criticizing her, but she didn't care. If she had to sit there for another one of Lila's looks, she was going to scream.

To her surprise, Elizabeth was in the kitchen, sitting at the table. "Why aren't you out celebrating with your team?" Jessica snapped as she opened the refrigerator and started pulling out sodas.

"Celebrating what?" Elizabeth sounded tired and depressed.

"Your precious football," Jessica said. "I suppose you think you're going to win now."

"We don't have the football," Elizabeth said quietly. "Mr. Henkel took it back."

Jessica stared at her twin. Her first impulse was to ask why. But she could tell from Elizabeth's expression that she was in no mood to talk.

Besides, it didn't matter why. They didn't have the football either, and that was all that mattered. Jessica raced back up to her room with the sodas.

"Guess what?" she announced quietly. "Elizabeth doesn't have the football! She gave it back to Mr. Henkel!"

Three sets of eyebrows shot up. "You're kidding!" Ellen exclaimed. "Then they don't have a chance!"

Even Lila looked satisfied. "That's good news. At least there's no way they'll win now."

Jessica happily agreed, and handed out the sodas. She couldn't honestly say she was back on top of the world. But at least she'd crawled up from the bottom.

Elizabeth's group spent the next couple of days following up leads.

"My aunt's got an attic filled with stuff she's

saved for years," Amy told them. "Maybe we can find something there."

So they spent an entire evening searching through Amy's aunt's attic. But they didn't find anything related to the sixties.

Then Julie remembered seeing something at the junk shop—a collection of souvenir plates from a World's Fair that had taken place in the sixties. The next day after school, they went tearing back to the shop. The plates were still there—but they cost two hundred dollars.

"I can't sell you just one," the lady told them apologetically. "It's part of a set, and it's very valuable."

George wasn't much help in their search. He didn't even seem interested anymore. Elizabeth had one faint hope—that Mr. Henkel would change his mind and call his son. But she knew that wasn't likely. Mr. Henkel was a very proud man. And if he believed that his son had rejected the football, he wasn't going to offer it again.

On Thursday, they gave up. "We have to turn everything in today," Elizabeth told her teammates. "The judges have to examine everything before the ceremony on Saturday, when they dedicate the dugouts. That's when they'll announce the winner."

Nobody said, ". . . and it won't be us," but that's what they were all thinking.

"Well, we tried," Julie said.

"I didn't," George said glumly. "I think I blew it for all of us."

"That's not true," Elizabeth told him firmly. "You did what you had to do."

"That's right," Julie said, and Amy agreed, too. George gave them a small smile.

"Thanks," he whispered.

"And we're all going to the ceremony together," Elizabeth announced. "Who knows? Maybe the judges will be so impressed with the two things we submitted that they won't care if we don't have three."

"Absolutely!" Amy declared.

"That's a definite possibility," Julie echoed.

Elizabeth could tell that they didn't really believe that. They were all mainly interested in cheering up George.

But from the sadness in George's eyes, Elizabeth knew they weren't having much success.

Saturday morning was bright and warm, a perfect day for an outdoor ceremony.

"They're going to have all the items we collected for the contest on display," Elizabeth told her parents as they prepared to leave the house.

"That ought to bring back memories for some of the parents," Mrs. Wakefield said. "What did your team contribute?"

"An old textbook from Sweet Valley Junior High, and an autographed picture of President Kennedy. There was a third thing we were hoping to get, but it didn't work out."

"Well, you made a fine contribution anyway," her father assured her. "Now, where's your sister? We want to have some time to look at all those things you kids collected before the ceremony starts."

"I'll get her," Elizabeth said, and went upstairs to Jessica's room. As she expected, her sister was still fixing herself up in front of the mirror.

"C'mon, Jess, we're ready to go."

Jessica gave her hair one last brush. "I want to look absolutely perfect," she declared. "They're going to take pictures of the winners, remember?"

Elizabeth remembered all too well. "You already look perfect," she said. She caught a glimpse of herself in the mirror, and pushed a stray lock of hair out of her eyes. Not that it mattered how she looked. No one was going to be taking her picture.

When Jessica was finally ready, the whole family piled into their maroon van and drove over to the school. Elizabeth had arranged to meet her team by the exhibit, and they were all there, including George. The items were set up on several tables in the center of the softball field, and the air was filled with conversation and laughter as students and families looked over the collection.

"Good grief, what's that?" Elizabeth asked. "It looks like a mound of hair."

Amy read the card that was attached to it. "'Beatles wig, 1964.' I guess people wore them so they'd look like the Beatles."

Farther down the table, they saw a photograph of the Beatles and ticket stubs from a Beatles concert.

"There's Jessica's team's stuff," Julie announced from farther down the table. "They have some interesting things," she commented.

Amy sniffed. "They have a Beatles album. Big deal. Everybody's got Beatles stuff."

"It's still a good collection," Elizabeth said loyally. No matter what nasty schemes Jessica pulled, she was still her sister, and she had to stand up for her.

"Ours is better," Julie insisted. "Our things are more important. The textbook stands for education, and the photograph stands for government."

"That's true," Elizabeth admitted. But two great items wouldn't win the contest for them.

"Attention!" a voice boomed out over the field. Elizabeth saw Mr. Clark, the principal, standing at a microphone. "Will everyone please take a seat in the stands so we may begin our program."

Elizabeth, Amy, George, and Julie took seats. Down the row from them, she saw Jessica and her team. They were all examining themselves in mirrors.

As the crowd settled down in the bleachers, Mr.

Clark began. "In celebration of Sweet Valley Middle School's twenty-fifth anniversary, we are burying a time capsule containing items from the sixties. Our students have been holding a competition to see which team could bring in the three most distinctive items representing that time. As you saw from the display, we have a very fine collection, and the judges have had a difficult time making a decision."

Behind him, Elizabeth could see three teachers examining the items on the table. Mr. Clark beckoned them to the microphone to announce their decision.

Just as he was about to step aside and hand the microphone to one of the judges, something seemed to catch his eye. He was looking at the entrance to the field. Following his gaze, Elizabeth turned to look in that direction and saw a figure in a wheelchair heading onto the field toward Mr. Clark.

"It's my father!" George exclaimed.

"And he's got the football," Elizabeth said, gasping.

A murmur went through the crowd as Mr. Clark covered the microphone with his hand and spoke with Mr. Henkel. Then the judges joined them. Then Mr. Clark spoke into the microphone.

"Would George Henkel please come down here?"

Elizabeth turned to George. He got up and made his way down to the field, his face pale.

"What's going on?" Amy asked in bewilderment.

Elizabeth felt a thrill shoot through her. "I don't know, " she said. "But I have a feeling it's something good!"

Ten

◇

No one spoke as Mr. Clark handed the microphone to Mr. Henkel and Mr. Henkel moved closer to speak into it.

"I hope you all will excuse this interruption. But I have something important to say, and I want everyone to hear it."

He held up the football so they could see it. "Some of you may remember me from twenty-five years ago, when I caught this ball during Sweet Valley Junior High's first championship game. That was a big moment for me."

He paused, and even from a distance Elizabeth could tell that this was difficult for him. He turned and looked for a moment at George, who was standing by his side. Then he continued speaking.

"A lot has happened since then. I'm not the man I used to be. And I've had a hard time dealing

98   SWEET VALLEY TWINS

with that. I've wasted a lot of time feeling sorry for myself."

He paused again, and lowered his head. When he looked up, he was smiling. "You know, this football was very special to me. And when my son asked if his team could have it for their project, I said no. I didn't want to part with it, because it was the only thing I had to remind me of better days. I said it was the most important thing in my life. Well, I was wrong. There's a person who is much more important to me. My son, George."

Elizabeth clutched Amy's hand. She felt an enormous lump forming in her throat.

Now Mr. Henkel's voice was trembling. "This football is only a memory. It's time for me to stop looking back, and start looking ahead. That's why I'm giving it to my son, with the hope that we can start making a future together."

He held the football out to George. George took it, held it for a moment, and then handed it to a judge, who placed it on the table with the other things. And then, despite the fact that a whole audience was watching, George threw his arms around his father.

For a moment, there was total silence. Then, suddenly, everyone was applauding. Elizabeth, Amy, and Julie all hugged each other. "That's the most beautiful thing I ever saw," Amy cried.

Elizabeth tried to wipe away her own tears. Seeing George and Mr. Henkel embracing was exactly what she had hoped for.

George wheeled his father away from the microphone to the edge of the stands and sat down beside him. Then Mr. Clark returned to the microphone.

"Thank you, Mr. Henkel, not only for giving us the football, but for reminding us what's really important in life. Now, I believe the judges have reached a decision. Mrs. Arnette?"

He stepped aside so the social studies teacher could speak into the microphone.

"First of all, I want to congratulate all the teams who participated in the time capsule project. Because of your efforts, students in twenty-five years will know what the 1960s were like in Sweet Valley.

"We judges did not have an easy time picking the winners. In deciding which collection of items was the finest, we did not look for the most unusual, or the most expensive. We wanted to see items which best represent what we at Sweet Valley Middle School believe in—yesterday, today, and tomorrow."

"The winning team members are Elizabeth Wakefield, Amy Sutton, Julie Porter, and George Henkel."

The applause was so deafening that Elizabeth could barely hear her own squeal of joy. The three girls leaped up, hugged each other, and then ran down the bleachers to where George was sitting with his father. Elizabeth spoke first. "We wouldn't have won without you, Mr. Henkel. Thank you."

"Thank *you*, Elizabeth," Mr. Henkel said. "Because of you, I've got my son back."

It was all Elizabeth could do to keep from crying. Hearing those words meant more to her than all the time capsules in the world.

As the applause died down, Mrs. Arnette began speaking again. "I'd like to ask the members of the winning team to step forward and tell us about each item, and what they mean to them."

"Oh my gosh!" Amy whispered. "I didn't know we'd have to give a speech!" But they all joined Mrs. Arnette at the microphone, and Julie went first. She picked up the photograph and held it high.

"This is a signed photograph of President Kennedy, the first president elected in the 1960s. To us, this photo represents leadership."

With a little push from Elizabeth, Amy went next. She held up the book. "This is a textbook that was used by one of the first classes at Sweet Valley Junior High. It's a symbol of education, and it stands for our belief in our school."

As Amy stepped aside, Elizabeth took George's hand and the two of them went to the microphone together. Elizabeth spoke first. "This football is a symbol of teamwork. It stands for working together to accomplish a goal."

Then George took a deep breath and spoke. "And it's a symbol of something passed on from one generation to the next. It stands for our belief in our parents."

Once again, applause swept over the bleachers. Only this time, the crowd stood up.

"It's a standing ovation!" Elizabeth exclaimed. And it seemed to go on forever.

Then a photographer came forward to take their pictures. "Does anyone have a mirror?" Julie asked anxiously. Elizabeth produced one, and they all spent a few moments frantically fixing their hair. Then the photographer took a photo of each of them, and another of the whole group.

Elizabeth felt like she was walking on air. What a day! She was so dazed, she was barely aware of the dugout dedication going on. As soon as it was over, she looked for her parents.

She found them shaking hands with Mr. Henkel.

There were more hugs, more congratulations. And then Elizabeth saw her sister coming toward them. She eyed Jessica a little nervously. Jessica didn't look upset at all, though. She congratulated Elizabeth, and then stepped back, looking at her critically.

"I'm glad you brushed your hair."

"Why?" Elizabeth asked.

"I wanted your picture to come out nicely, because in twenty-five years, people will be looking at it. And who knows?" Jessica grinned mischievously. "They just might think it's me!"

Eleven

◇

It was a week after the contest and Elizabeth was still basking in the glow of the time capsule victory. She hurried home after school, clutching a red folder tightly in her hand. It was an essay she had written for her English class, and it was one of the most difficult papers she had ever written. She had revised it three times

But all her hard work paid off. The essay had been returned that day, and she had received an A plus! She couldn't wait to tell her family.

"Mom!" she called as she ran in the door. "Mom, guess what?"

But there was no answer. Elizabeth sighed in disappointment. Her mother was probably still at work. She checked the refrigerator door for a note, but there was no message.

Elizabeth helped herself to some cookies and milk, and sat down at the kitchen table. It seemed to her that her mother had been working more than usual lately. She was hardly ever home when the twins got home from school.

The house was so silent that when the phone rang, Elizabeth jumped. *That's probably Mom,* she thought as she got up to answer it. "Hello," she called into the phone.

"Hi, honey. Let me talk to your mother." It was Mr. Wakefield.

"She's not here."

There was a brief silence on the other end. "Do you know where she is?"

Elizabeth glanced around the kitchen to make sure she hadn't overlooked a note. "No, she didn't leave any message."

She could hear her father sigh over the phone.

"I have to take a client out to dinner, and I wanted her to join us."

"I'll tell her to call you as soon as she gets home," Elizabeth offered.

"It doesn't matter," Mr. Wakefield said. "I'll just take him out by myself. I'll see you later, honey."

That's odd, Elizabeth thought as she hung up the phone. *Dad almost always knows where Mom is.* And she'd never heard of her father going out to dinner without her mother.

Just then, Jessica came in through the back door. "Where's Mom?" she asked Elizabeth breathlessly. "We're supposed to go shopping."

"She's not here," Elizabeth told her. "I don't know where she is."

Jessica frowned. "This isn't like her to break a promise."

"Maybe she's just late getting back from work," Elizabeth suggested.

Jessica sat down and drummed her fingernails on the table. "She's *always* working late these days. What 's going on? Did everyone in Sweet Valley decide to redecorate their houses at the same time?"

"It seems like it," Elizabeth agreed. "I feel like I hardly see Mom at all anymore."

"I saw her at the mall yesterday," Jessica said. "But she didn't see me."

Elizabeth was surprised. "What was she doing there?"

"She was on her way into a restaurant with some man."

"Maybe it was someone who's having his house decorated," Elizabeth said.

"Then why weren't they at his house?" Jessica demanded.

Elizabeth was puzzled, too. "I don't know, Jess. Maybe they were taking a break. Are you sure you don't know who she was with?"

"I'm positive," Jessica said. "It wasn't one of Mom and Dad's friends. I've never seen him before." Then she grinned. "Maybe Mom has a secret boyfriend."

Elizabeth was shocked. "Jess! That's not funny!"

"I was just kidding," Jessica said quickly. She took a cookie and bit into it. The two girls sat eating in silence for a minute. Then Jessica looked at Elizabeth thoughtfully. "Have you noticed that Mom and Dad haven't been spending much time together lately?"

Elizabeth *had* noticed that, but she didn't want to think about it. "I guess they've both been very busy with work," she murmured lamely.

"*Maybe*," Jessica said darkly. "But it's weird."

Elizabeth gazed at her in alarm. "What do you mean, weird?"

"Well, Mom's hardly ever around these days. And who was that man she was with? Just between us, I think something strange is going on."

And Elizabeth, feeling troubled, could only agree.

What is Mrs. Wakefield up to? Find out in Sweet Valley Twins #24, **JUMPING TO CONCLUSIONS.**